A Christmas Tree

❈ *in the* ❈

White House

Gary Hines   illustrated by Alexandra Wallner

Henry Holt and Company ❦ New York

Henry Holt and Company, Inc., *Publishers since 1866,* 115 West 18th Street, New York, New York 10011
Henry Holt is a registered trademark of Henry Holt and Company, Inc.

Published in Canada by Fitzhenry & Whiteside Ltd., 195 Allstate Parkway, Markham, Ontario L3R 4T8.

Permission for the use of the photograph on page 30 courtesy of the Free Library of Philadelphia

Library of Congress Cataloging-in-Publication Data
Hines, Gary. A Christmas tree in the White House / Gary Hines; illustrated by Alexandra Wallner.
Summary: President Theodore Roosevelt does not approve of cutting down living trees just to be used as
Christmas decorations, but his two young sons try to sneak one into the White House anyway.
1. Roosevelt, Theodore, 1858-1919—Juvenile fiction. [1. Roosevelt, Theodore, 1858-1919—Fiction. 2. Christmas trees—Fiction.
3. Conservation of natural resources—Fiction.] I. Wallner, Alexandra, ill. II. Title. PZ7.H5725Ch 1998 [E]—dc21 97-50416

ISBN 0-8050-5076-0 First Edition—1998 Printed in the United States of America on acid-free paper. ∞
10 9 8 7 6 5 4 3 2 1 The artist used gouache on 140-lb. Arches cold-press paper to create the illustrations for this book.

For Anna —G.H.

To Margery, with love and many thanks —A.W.

President Roosevelt dashed down the hallway, his six children tumbling behind him.

"Bully!" cried the president, leaping around the obstacle course of chairs.

Womp! A pillow went sailing over his head.

"Missed!" yelled the boys.

"I'll get you now!" the president hollered. "Charge!"

Squeals of laughter bounced off the walls as the children toppled onto the floor with their father.

Theodore Roosevelt jumped up. "I surrender!" he yelled.

"We win!" cried Archie.

The giggles died down as Alice, Theodore Junior, Kermit, Ethel, Archie, and Quentin caught their breath.

"Papa?"

"Yes?"

"When are we going to get our tree? Christmas is almost here."

"Well," said President Roosevelt, "I've been thinking about that. It's not good to cut down trees for mere decoration. We must set a good example for the people of America. Our evergreen trees must be allowed to grow. I've decided there will be no Christmas tree in the White House this year."

"But Papa!" whined Quentin. "We've always had a Christmas tree. Christmas won't be the same without one."

"I'm sorry, but my conservation work is very important. We must save our trees for the future."

"Please, Papa!" begged the children.

"No!" said the president. Then wriggling his fingers, he began to tickle them until they raced to their rooms, squealing with laughter.

The next day, the two youngest boys, Quentin and Archie, went to talk to their aunt Anna about the Christmas tree.

"No tree in the White House? What a shame!" she said. "But maybe something can be done."

"We have an idea," said the boys. They leaned close and whispered in her ear.

The next evening, after it had grown dark, a lone window in the back of the White House opened. Two small heads poked out in the chilly night.

"Brrr!" Quentin said.

"There it is," Archie whispered, "right where Auntie left it."

"How can we move it inside?" Quentin asked. "Should we carry it?"

"No, that'll make too much noise. I've got a better idea. Remember when we played that escape game with Papa, and he lowered us out the window with a rope? We could make one out of our sheets."

Quentin's face lit up. "Oh! That's a good idea."

The boys scampered to their beds and tied some sheets together to make a rope. Then, while Archie went outside, Quentin went back to the window. The cold winter air made him shiver. He peered into the blackness. "Are you there, Archie?"

"Yes. Now hurry up! It's freezing." Holding on to one end of the rope, Quentin lowered the other end to his brother.

Archie worked fast, tying it around the tree. "It's ready to go," he said. "I'll be right there." As soon as Archie got back to the room, both boys pulled the little tree through the open window.

Tap. Tap. Tap.

"Listen! What's that?" asked Quentin.

"Footsteps!" Archie said. "Quick! We must hide the tree!"

They scrunched the branches and hurriedly shoved the tree under the Archie's bed.

The door opened. "I thought I heard something in here," their father said. "Shouldn't you two be getting ready for bed?"

"We're not sleepy, Papa," answered Quentin.

"Hmmm." The president rocked back on his heels, then sniffed. "What's that I smell?"

Quentin gulped.

"Uh, well . . . the window," Archie explained. "We've had it open for a while . . . to see the stars. Maybe it's something from outside."

"Yes, the window," Quentin agreed, his eyes big.

President Roosevelt nodded slowly. "Could be," he finally said. "Now I suggest you boys get into your pajamas."

Quentin and Archie watched their father leave, then dropped to their knees and pulled out the tree.

"It got squashed," Quentin moaned.

"Don't worry, it'll be okay," Archie said. "Let's put it in the closet."

"Good idea!" Quentin whispered. "Maybe we should go get the others!"

"No, they'd tell! Especially Alice."

Quentin nodded.

The boys hauled the tree across the room.
Tap. Tap. Tap.
More footsteps.
"Oh, no! That sounds like Mama!" cried Quentin.

Quickly they flopped the tree on Archie's bed, threw a blanket over it, and pounced on top just as their mother came to the door. "Aren't you in your pajamas yet?"

"Almost," Quentin said, wiggling to get more comfortable. "We'll sleep like logs tonight."

Archie gave him an elbow.

Mrs. Roosevelt's eyes narrowed. "All right then. Good night."

"Good night, Mama," the boys said, blowing her kisses.

They listened until the footsteps disappeared. Then they jumped down, uncovered the tree, and carried it to the closet.

First, they stuck the trunk in a box of sand so the tree could stand by itself. Next, they got out the paper chains and stars they'd made earlier and hung them on the branches. Finally, they wrapped some boxes with pretty paper to make them look like gifts.

"There!" Archie cried. "Look at our beautiful tree! It sure smells like Christmas in here."

KNOCK . . . KNOCK . . . KNOCK!

top secret stuff

Quentin gasped.

"Quick, shut the door!" Archie whispered. He stood in front
of the closet, trying to look innocent as their father stepped into
the room.

The president took a long sniff and marched over to the closet.
He flung open the door and glared at the little tree.

Folding his arms, he turned and eyed the boys.

Archie and Quentin squirmed.

"Get your shoes on," he said sternly. "We're going to see the chief forester. If you won't listen to me, perhaps you'll listen to him. He'll set you straight on this."

"But isn't it too late?" Archie asked.

"Oh, he'll be up," their father answered.

President Roosevelt steered the boys out of the White House, down the street,

and into the home of his good friend Gifford Pinchot.

"Please explain to these boys why Christmas trees are not a good idea. They go against all my conservation efforts!"

Gifford Pinchot leaned back in his chair and looked at the president. Then he looked at the boys' sad faces. The ends of his thick mustache twitched.

"I'm afraid I can't do that," he said.

"Why not?" the president asked.

"Because sometimes, if done right, it is a good idea to cut some of the young trees," the forester explained. "It gives the others more sunlight and room to grow bigger and stronger."

"Really?" asked the president.

"Really," said Pinchot.

The president thought for a moment. "Well, that puts a new twist on things, doesn't it?" Then he smiled. "Isn't that bully!"

"Hoorah!" shouted Archie.

"Bully!" cried Quentin.

Everyone laughed.

Christmas Day finally came to the White House. Aunt Anna arrived early in the morning with a tiny star for the tree. Archie led her to the boys' bedroom, where the tree now stood in the center of the room. The rest of the family crowded around. Aunt Anna had presents for everyone, even Jack the dog, Tom Quartz the kitten, and Algonquin the pony.

"Merry Christmas!" shouted the president.

"Merry Christmas!" shouted the boys. "Hooray for the tree!"

About Theodore Roosevelt

Theodore Roosevelt was the twenty-sixth president of the United States and, at age forty-two, the youngest. When William McKinley was assassinated in 1901, the energetic Roosevelt, then vice president, assumed office. A man once remarked that "there was such fun in being led by him."

During President Roosevelt's administration, the Panama Canal was constructed and laws were passed to improve the quality of food in the United States. He organized reforms that kept big business from getting too big. His belief in the rights of the "little man" endeared him to many people. Not everyone liked Roosevelt, though, and some referred to him as "that cowboy in the White House." Nevertheless, he returned to office by a wide margin of votes in 1904 and remained president until 1909.

A strong conservationist, Roosevelt worked closely with his chief forester and good friend, Gifford Pinchot. Together, they set aside millions of acres of forested land for future use and protection. Within these forests are many of the nation's precious natural resources.

About the Story

Not all the details in this story are true. The times between events have been shortened, and the conversations are made up. But the "hiding" of the Christmas tree in the closet did happen. And one of the boys' aunts, possibly President Roosevelt's sister, Anna, did feel sorry for Quentin and Archie. How the boys snuck the tree inside is unknown, but their father eventually found out and sent them to see Gifford Pinchot. Because of Pinchot's advice, Roosevelt still forbade a large tree in the White House. But he did let the boys keep a small one in Archie and Quentin's bedroom.

About the Children

President Roosevelt loved to play with his children. He read to them all the time and knew plenty of ghost stories. Once, when he was governor of New York, he pretended the governor's mansion was being attacked by enemies. He used a rope to lower his children out of a window to safety.

Pillow fights and obstacle courses in the White House halls were not uncommon either. There were overnight camping trips and picnics, too. President Roosevelt let the children and their friends swim with their clothes on and led them on hikes from which they all came back dirty and ragged. "To be with him was to have fun," remembered a cousin. Roosevelt once wondered if he, as president, was being a bit "undignified" with his wild and playful antics. Such doubts were short-lived, however, for as he wrote, "I love all these children and have great fun with them, and am touched by the way in which they feel that I am their special friend, champion, and companion."